Elisa
the Royal
Adventure
Fairy

Special thanks to Rachel Elliot

ISBN 978-0-545-43393-8

12 11 10 9 8 7 6 5 4 3 2 1   12 13 14 15 16 17/0

Printed in China   68
First Scholastic printing, August 2012

Elisa
the Royal Adventure Fairy

by Daisy Meadows

SCHOLASTIC INC.

New York   Toronto   London   Auckland
Sydney   Mexico City   New Delhi   Hong Kong

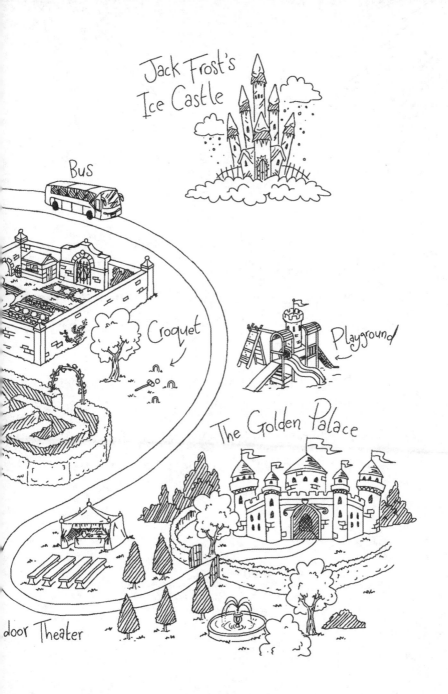

Jack Frost's
Ice Castle

Bus

Croquet

Playground

The Golden Palace

door Theater

The fairies are planning a magical ball,
With guests of honor and fun for all.
They're expecting a night full of laughter and cheer,
But they'll get a shock when my goblins appear!

Adventures and treats will be things of the past,
And I'll beat those troublesome fairies at last.
My iciest magic will blast through the room
And the world will be plunged into grimness
and gloom!

Contents

A Ghostly Surprise

"I wonder what adventures Louis and Caroline have planned for us tonight," said Kirsty Tate, smiling across the grand banquet table at her best friend, Rachel Walker.

It was spring vacation, and they were staying at the Golden Palace for the Royal Sleepover Camp, a special week-long event for kids. Louis and Caroline were two of the palace's camp directors, and they had been looking after the kids all week, making sure the activities were fit for princes and princesses.

"I'm sure they've planned something wonderful," said Rachel, scraping the last bit of strawberry ice cream from her silver bowl. The grand banquet hall looked very beautiful, decorated with lots of twinkling candles and lights. Kirsty gazed thoughtfully out the large round window at the end of the hall. It was twilight, but she could still see the silhouette of the palace's crumbling old tower. It looked majestic

against the purple sky, and it was the only place that the campers were not allowed to go.

"I wish they would let us climb all the way up to the top of the tower," Kirsty said. "I'd love to explore up there!"

"It sounds kind of scary to me," said a girl named Victoria, who was sitting next to Kirsty. "I'm not very adventurous."

Rachel and Kirsty exchanged a secret smile. They'd already had plenty of adventures that week! They had been helping their friends the Princess Fairies get their magic tiaras back from Jack Frost and his goblins. So far, they had found the tiaras that belonged to Princess Hope the Happiness Fairy, Princess Cassidy the Costume Fairy, and Princess Anya the Cuddly Creatures Fairy. But there were still four more tiaras to find.

Each of the Princess Fairies looked after a special kind of fairy magic. Without the magical tiaras, things would go wrong in both the human and fairy worlds. Jack Frost and his mischievous goblins had stolen the tiaras during a ball at the Fairyland Palace, then brought them to the human world. Queen Titania had not been able to stop them from taking the tiaras, but she had used her magic to make sure that the magical crowns would be hidden at the Golden Palace. Now the fairies were depending on Rachel and Kirsty to help them find the tiaras.

Just then, Victoria gave a cry of surprise. "Look!" she exclaimed. "Why didn't we notice that before?"

There was a tall vase in the center of the banquet table, containing long-stemmed pink roses. But Victoria had noticed that there was something tucked among the roses—a mysterious scroll. She leaned forward for a closer look and read:

"Ooh, it must be about tonight's activity!" said Rachel excitedly. "Quick, open it!"

Victoria pulled the scroll from the vase, being careful not to damage any of the rose petals. She unrolled it and everyone gathered around her to see what it said. The instructions were written in large gold letters.

Meet us where adventures flow
Among the pages white as snow.
A room containing tales of glory
Within each bound and printed story.

"That sounds pretty complicated," said a boy named Arthur.

"I hope it isn't anything too hard," said Victoria. Rachel and Kirsty exchanged a surprised glance. The other kids had seemed to enjoy their activities and adventures. But now they weren't even interested in solving the riddle!

"Pages and printed stories," said Rachel. "What room contains those things? Oh, I know! The library!"

"You're right!" said Kirsty. "Come on, I'll bet they're waiting for us there."

The kids left the banquet hall and walked across the polished entrance area to the foot of the main staircase.

Flickering candles lit their way as they walked slowly up toward the library. Suddenly, Victoria and Arthur stopped in their tracks. Arthur turned white, and Victoria raised a trembling hand to point to a shadow on the wall.

"It's a g-ghost!" she squeaked.

Everyone except Kirsty and Rachel shrieked at one another. The girls caught a fleeting glimpse of a dark shape, but then it vanished.

"Did you see that?" asked Kirsty.

Rachel nodded. "I couldn't tell what it

was, though," she said. "It disappeared too quickly."

"It was a ghost," said Arthur in a terrified whisper. "A ghost of a king from long ago who used to stay here."

"I'm sure it couldn't really have been a ghost," said Rachel sensibly.

"It was probably just a weird shadow from the candle flames," Kirsty added.

They both felt a little surprised that the other kids were so scared!

"Let's run the rest of the way!" cried Victoria in a shaky voice.

Behind the Bookcase

They all hurried up the stairs and
darted into the library. It was lined with
bookcases made of polished oak, and the
lamps around the room were burning
brightly. On a rug in the middle of the
room, a large cloth covered a mysterious
pile. But the palace camp directors were
nowhere to be seen.

"Where are Louis and Caroline?"
asked Kirsty, looking around.

"M-maybe the ghost has taken them to the tower," stammered Arthur. "M-maybe they know that it's haunted, and that's why we're not allowed up there!"

A squeaking sound made them jump, and then one of the bookcases began to move. It spun around and everyone shrieked . . . then burst into laughter. Caroline and Louis were right in front of them!

"Sorry to scare you all," chuckled Louis. "We thought you might like to see one of our secret hiding places!"

"How does it work?" asked Rachel in excitement.

Louis showed them a vase on one of the shelves.

"This isn't really a vase at all," he explained. "It's a secret lever!"

He tipped the vase toward him by its neck, and the bookcase spun around again, taking Louis with it. They heard him laugh on the other side of the bookcase, and

then it turned and brought him back into the library.

"It's a wonderful trick," said Kirsty. "I wish we had one of those at home!"

"I hope we didn't scare you," said Caroline.

"It's just that we had a fright on the main staircase," Victoria explained.

When the directors heard what the kids had seen, Caroline shook her head with a smile. "I promise you, there's no such thing as ghosts," she said. "What

you saw was probably the shadows of clouds moving across the moon."

"We thought that the ghost might have taken you to the tower," Arthur whispered. "We guessed it was haunted."

"The tower isn't haunted," Caroline assured him. "But it's very old and some of the steps are missing, so that's why we ask you not to go up there."

"Now," said Louis in a cheerful voice, "get into pairs, everyone."

Rachel clasped Kirsty's hand. They

watched as Louis and Caroline pulled away the cloth on the rug. Underneath was a pile of party bags.

"Help yourselves. One bag per pair," said Caroline.

Rachel and Kirsty excitedly chose a bag and peeked inside. It contained two flashlights, a small scroll, and two crowns.

"All the crowns are missing their jewels," Louis explained. "Tonight's activity is a treasure hunt around the palace to find the jewels!"

The kids gave little gasps of excitement, and Louis grinned at them.

"You'll find some clues on the scrolls," he said. "By following the clues, you will find the missing jewel stickers to complete your crowns. The clues for each pair are different, so you will be spread around the palace. The first team to collect all their jewels and return to the library is the winner. Good luck!"

The children headed out into the corridor. Rachel and Kirsty felt very excited, but everyone else looked kind of down.

"I'm not very good at solving clues," they heard one boy mutter.

"I wish I could read a book instead," Victoria said.

"Well, I can't wait to get started!" said Rachel. She pulled out the scroll and read the first clue to Kirsty. "Look for something that protects a knight in battle, then search behind the lion."

"Something that protects a knight in battle," Kirsty repeated. "It must be some kind of armor."

"Remember the armory we visited on the first day?" Rachel said eagerly. "Let's start our search there."

Rachel and Kirsty hurried to the armory. Inside, suits of armor stood at attention, all in a row. The walls were hung with heavy tapestries that told the stories of ancient battles. In the center of the room was a display of antique shields, all painted with brightly colored pictures.

"Kirsty, I think our clue is telling us to look behind a shield!" said Rachel. "A shield protects a knight in battle. I

bet that one of these shields has a lion painted on it!"

The girls rushed forward to examine the shields one by one, looking carefully at all the pictures.

"A unicorn . . . a bear . . . an eagle . . ." said Kirsty, moving along one side of the display.

"A wolf . . . a panther . . . a LION!" exclaimed Rachel. "Here it is!"

Jewel
Trackers

Together, Kirsty and Rachel looked
behind the shield for a jewel sticker.

"There isn't anything there," said
Kirsty, disappointed. "We must have
read the clue wrong."

Rachel looked all around the armory.

"There's nothing else here with a lion
on it," she said. "I don't understand."

"Come on," said Kirsty. "Let's go
back to the library and ask Louis and
Caroline if we made a mistake."

They walked out of the armory and bumped into Arthur and Victoria, who were looking very frustrated.

"Hello," said Rachel. "Did you find your first jewel yet?"

"No," Arthur said angrily. "These clues are silly."

"We solved the clue, but we couldn't find the jewel sticker," said Victoria.

"Same here," Kirsty told her.

"I'm not sure I want to keep doing the treasure hunt if  it's going to be this hard," said Victoria with a sigh.

"Don't give up yet," said Rachel. "I'm sure we just have to think about the

clues again. After all, treasure hunts aren't supposed to be too easy."

"OK," said Arthur, looking a little more cheerful. "Come on, Victoria, I have another idea."

He hurried down the wide corridor, and Rachel and Kirsty looked at each other.

"It's strange that everyone seems so ready to give up, isn't it?" said Kirsty thoughtfully.

"Everyone except us!" Rachel replied

with a grin. "Come on, where should we look next?"

They headed down the hall in the opposite direction. Night had fallen, and small lamps jutted out of the thick stone wall, giving off a warm orange glow. There was a narrow window cut into the wall ahead of them, and the light there seemed to be flickering.

"Is one of the lamps going out?" Rachel wondered.

The girls hurried over to the window and had a wonderful surprise. Princess Elisa the Royal Adventure Fairy was hovering in the opening! Dressed in her silky pants and a sparkly tank top, she looked even more beautiful than they had remembered.

"Hello, Rachel! Hello, Kirsty!" she said in a tinkling voice. "It's wonderful to see you again."

"It's good to see you, too, Princess Elisa," said Kirsty eagerly. "We're in the middle of a treasure hunt, but I think something has gone wrong. We were supposed to

find jewel stickers for our crowns, but they're not where the clues say they should be."

Elisa nodded sadly. "I know," she said. "The treasure hunt has gone wrong because my tiara is still missing. That's why I came here tonight—we must find the tiara, or it won't just be the treasure hunt that goes wrong."

"What do you mean?" Rachel gasped.

"My tiara helps me protect everyone's sense of adventure," Elisa explained. "If I don't get it back, no one will ever want to do anything brave or try anything new again!"

"That explains why the other boys and girls aren't very excited about the treasure hunt," said Kirsty.

"And they were all really scared by the shadow on the staircase in the main hall," agreed Rachel. "But Elisa, why aren't we affected? Kirsty and I feel just as adventurous as ever!"

Elisa pointed to the lockets that hung around the girls' necks.

"Your lockets contain magical fairy dust," she said. "That has protected your sense of adventure. Plus you have already helped three of the other princesses, so their magic protects you, too!"

Just then, something on the floor sparkled and caught Rachel's eye.

"Look, a jewel sticker!" she cried, stooping to pick it up. "It's a ruby. This must be one of the missing stickers for the crowns!"

"Something else is sparkling over there," said Kirsty, hurrying forward. "Yes, it's another jewel sticker! An emerald."

Suddenly, the lamps flickered and went out. The only light came from the moon that was shining through the narrow window.

"Rachel, weren't there some flashlights

in the party bag?" asked Kirsty.

Rachel pulled out the flashlights and handed one to Kirsty. They switched them on and pointed them at their floor. The yellow beams picked out another sticker sparkling a few steps away.

"It's a trail," said Elisa eagerly. "Let's follow it!"

The girls walked forward slowly, with
Elisa fluttering between them. Their
flashlights picked out another sticker,
and another, and another. Sparkling
diamonds, amethysts, and sapphires led
them down a long passageway, through
a tiny door and out onto an outdoor
walkway that ran along the front of the

palace. Stars glimmered in the indigo sky as they followed the stickers to the foot of a narrow, winding staircase. Rachel and Kirsty looked up and saw that they were standing beneath the crumbling tower.

"Why did you stop?" asked Elisa.

"We're not allowed to go up there," Kirsty explained. "The steps aren't safe to climb." The girls were very disappointed, but Elisa smiled. "You can fly up instead," she said. "Then you won't have to touch the steps at all!"

Elisa waved her wand, and a shower of silvery fairy dust sprinkled over the girls. Shimmering wings appeared on their backs and they shrank to fairy-size, as did their flashlights and party bag.

"Thank you!" said Rachel, fluttering into the air and twirling around in delight. "Now we can explore the tower without breaking the rules!"

Eagerly, the girls and Elisa zoomed up the winding staircase. Then, suddenly, a strange shadow loomed over them!

"Quick, hide!" cried Elisa.

They ducked into an arrow-slit cut into the wall and held their breath. The ghost came closer and closer . . . and then a green foot appeared on the stairs above them. It wasn't a ghost — it was a goblin trudging down the stairs!

"*More* jewel stickers," he was grumbling under his breath. "I've spent all day looking for jewel stickers, and now Jack Frost wants even *more*! He gets to play King of the Golden Palace and boss us around all the time. It's not fair!"

"So the tower isn't haunted," whispered Rachel as the goblin stomped past in

a huff. "Jack
Frost and his
goblins are
hiding up
there!"

"Do you think
your tiara could
be there, too,
Elisa?" asked
Kirsty hopefully.

"We have to find out!" said Elisa in
a determined voice. "Come on!"

They darted out of their hiding place
and zoomed up until they reached a
heavy wooden door. On the other side,
someone was making a lot of noise.

"I recognize that voice!" Elisa
whispered to the girls.

"So do I," said Rachel, sounding

concerned. "It's Jack Frost!"

Kirsty noticed another arrow-slit farther along the wall.

"Let's fly outside the tower and try to find a way into the room," she suggested.

They flew out through the arrow-slit and saw that one of the walls had almost completely  crumbled away. They flicked off their tiny flashlights and peered over the rubble.

The room was faintly lit by three candles in a candelabra, and Jack Frost was sitting on a moth-eaten throne in the center. He had one leg crooked over the arm of the throne, and a beautiful tiara sat on top of his spiky head. It was much too small for him. As the girls watched, it slipped sideways and he shoved it back in place.

"Fetch me more jewels!" he was bellowing at the goblins in the room. "Bring me more cake! Sing me a song! Paint my portrait!"

The goblins were scurrying around in a panic. One was carrying a lopsided cake with gray icing, but he tripped. The cake flew through the air and landed at Jack Frost's feet with a loud *splat*.

"Fool!" roared Jack Frost, bouncing up and down in his seat. The tiara slid sideways again and dangled from his ear. "Bring me cake *now*!"

A goblin in a black beret was standing beside an easel, angrily waving a fistful of paintbrushes at a third goblin, who was stomping on tubes of paint, sending colored blobs squirting through the air.

In the corner, a very small goblin was strumming an out-of-tune guitar and squawking loudly.

"I think he's *singing*," said Rachel,

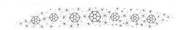

covering her hands with her ears. "I wish he'd stop!"

"No," said Kirsty, her eyes sparkling. "I've got an idea. It's very dark in there, and it's total chaos. Maybe with everything that's going on, Jack Frost won't notice us grabbing the tiara!"

"It's worth a try," said Elisa, always ready for adventure.

Moving cautiously, they flew through the hole in the wall toward Jack Frost, trying to keep to the shadows. They got closer and closer, and Rachel's heart was hammering. Soon they would be close enough to touch the tiara!

Suddenly, Jack Frost jerked his head to bark an order at a goblin, and Rachel jumped. Her finger accidentally pushed against the flashlight, switching the light on. The three fairies were lit up!

"Intruders!" Jack Frost howled in rage.

He fired an ice bolt at them, and poor Rachel was frozen solid, her flashlight in one

hand and the party bag in the other.

"Rachel!" cried Kirsty.

But before they could do anything to help her, Kirsty and Elisa were blasted back through the hole in the broken-down wall!

Tricky Fairies

Kirsty and Elisa were horrified. They
had to rescue Rachel and the tiara—but
how? They pressed themselves against
the outside wall of the tower, listening to
Jack Frost yelling at the goblins.

"Catch those pesky fairies *now*!" he
howled.

Kirsty and Elisa heard the thunder of large feet as the goblins hurried down

the tower. They were shrieking and grumbling as they slipped and scurried down the steps. "What are we going to do?" asked Elisa. "We have to keep the goblins out of the way if we're going to help Rachel—and get my tiara back."

Suddenly, Kirsty remembered the secret hiding place in the library.

"I've got an idea, but there's no time to explain," said Kirsty. "We just have to get the goblins to the library."

At that moment, the goblins tumbled out of the tower and onto the outdoor walkway. As they picked themselves up, Kirsty dove toward them.

"See if you can catch us!" she called to them.

She and Elisa zipped back into the palace, hearing yells of goblin rage behind them. They zoomed down the corridor, and the goblins

charged after them, puffing and panting as they ran.

Elisa led the goblins through side
passageways and unused rooms,
carefully avoiding the places where the
other campers might be. Kirsty flew
ahead of her, checking that each room
was free of kids and palace workers.
At last, they arrived at the library and
darted inside, just before the goblins
caught up with them.

"Quick, come and sit here!" said Kirsty as she perched on the revolving bookcase, next to the vase.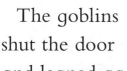

The goblins shut the door and leaned against it, panting.

"We've got you now," said the goblin with the beret. "You can't get away from us in here, you tricky fairies!"

"Come and get us, then," said Kirsty, her hand on the vase.

"What are you going to do?" asked Elisa.

"When I say 'Go,' fly forward as fast

as you can," Kirsty whispered.

The goblins charged toward them and, just at the right moment, Kirsty tipped the vase forward.

"Go!" she yelled.

As Elisa and Kirsty zoomed across the room, the bookcase whirled around and swooped the goblins into the hiding place behind it!

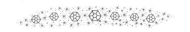

"It worked!" Kirsty exclaimed. "Now let's rescue Rachel—and your tiara, too."

They flew out of the palace and back up to the tower. Carefully, they peeked over the broken wall. They could see Rachel frozen in a block of ice on a table. Nearby, Jack Frost was vainly strutting around the tower room in a long yellow robe.

"I'm not sure that yellow suits my skin tone," they heard him mutter. "Maybe the blue would be better."

He tore off the yellow robe and

pulled on a dark-
blue velvet cape.
"Does this match
the tiara?" he
wondered aloud.
"If only I could
see which robe
makes me look the
most handsome."
"That gives me
an idea," said Kirsty.
"Elisa, can you use your magic to make
me into a goblin? If I bring Jack Frost
a mirror, maybe that will distract him
so that we can rescue Rachel and the
tiara."

"Oh, Kirsty, that sounds like a
wonderful plan," said Elisa with shining
eyes. "But it could be dangerous."

"I don't care," said Kirsty bravely. "My best friend is in there, and she needs my help!"

Elisa put her arms around Kirsty and gave her a warm hug.

"You're a very good friend," Elisa said. "I'll help however I can."

Kirsty and Elisa flew through the arrow-slit in the tower wall and landed in the hallway outside the room that Jack Frost was in. Elisa waved her wand over Kirsty's head and a wave of green sparkles sprinkled down on her.

"Skin of green and clumpy feet,
Fool Jack Frost with our deceit."

Kirsty grew back to human-size and felt her nose grow longer and longer. Her skin took on a greenish tint and her feet doubled in size. Elisa waved her wand again, and an ornate gold mirror appeared in Kirsty's hand. Kirsty held it up and saw a goblin face staring back at her. "Perfect!" she said with a hoarse goblin giggle.

Elisa fluttered into her pocket, and Kirsty knocked on the door. It flew open at once and Jack Frost stood scowling down at her.

"Well?" he snapped.

Kirsty felt a little scared, but then thought of Rachel.

"I brought you a mirror," she said in a gruff goblin voice.

A vain smile cracked Jack Frost's grumpy frown.

"Excellent!" he declared. "Now I can admire myself properly. Well, don't just stand there! Come in!"

A Sense of Adventure

Kirsty scurried into the room and went to stand by the candelabra. She held up the mirror so Jack Frost could see himself.

"Mirror, mirror, in your hand, who's the best in all the land?" he asked.

"Jack Frost, of course," said Kirsty, giving a deep bow.

He smirked and gazed at himself in the mirror. While he was distracted, Elisa slipped out of Kirsty's pocket. She fluttered over to the table and tapped her wand against the block of ice. It melted instantly, and Rachel was free.

"Thank you, Elisa!" she whispered, giving the little fairy a hug. But just then, Jack Frost spotted Elisa and Rachel in the mirror's reflection!

"Pesky fairies!" he snarled, lunging at them.

"Look out!" cried Kirsty.

"Traitor!" Jack Frost shouted.

He raised his wand, but Elisa was

faster. She quickly turned Kirsty back
into a fairy. Kirsty zipped
sideways and avoided the
ice bolt that Jack
Frost shot at
her.

Suddenly
they heard a
loud thumping
and thundering.
The goblins were
racing back up the
tower—they must have escaped
from behind the bookcase!

"Keep still!" roared Jack Frost
as Elisa and the girls fluttered around
him.

He shot another ice bolt at them,
and then had to clutch at the tiara

to stop it from falling off his head.

"We just have to get the tiara to slip off his head!" Rachel realized. "Quick—fly around the room as fast as you can!"

The three friends zoomed around the tower room so fast that they looked blurry to Jack Frost. Ice bolts hurtled

from his wand as he leaped into the air to try to catch them. His long fingers snatched at them, but the fairies stayed just out of his reach.

"Follow me!" cried Rachel.

She led Kirsty and Elisa around the back of the throne. As the door burst open and the goblins raced in, the girls darted out of the hole in the broken-down wall. They dropped immediately downward.

With a yell of rage, Jack Frost lunged at them. He thrust his head and shoulders over the broken wall and gazed down. He had forgotten all about the tiara on his head! It tumbled off and he gave an enraged roar as Elisa made a clean catch. It shrank to fairy-size at once.

"We did it!" cheered Rachel and Kirsty together. Jack Frost shook his fist at them as they fluttered down to the walkway. Elisa placed her tiara on her head, and turned to Rachel and Kirsty with sparkling eyes.

"You are very special friends," she said. "I can see that you both carry a sense of adventure in your hearts. Thank you for everything you've done."

"You're welcome," said Rachel with a big smile.

"It was definitely the most exciting adventure yet!" Kirsty added.

Elisa returned the girls to human-size, and then flicked her wand in the air. A flurry of sparkling jewels flew from the tip and zoomed into the palace through every door and window.

"I have put new jewel stickers all around the palace," said Elisa. "The treasure hunt can go ahead!"

She blew them both little fairy kisses and then disappeared in a tiny, glittering whirlwind. Rachel and Kirsty smiled at each other, and then Rachel looked up at the tower.

"I don't think Jack Frost will be causing any more trouble tonight," she said with a laugh. "Come on, let's go and finish the treasure hunt!"

An hour later, all the kids were back in the library, and the room was filled with laughter and chatter. Rachel and Kirsty put the final jewel sticker on their crowns and held them up to the light.

"They look beautiful!" said a girl named Harriet, holding up her own crown. "What do you think of mine?"

"It's really pretty," said Rachel with a smile.

Victoria and Arthur had been the first to find all their jewel stickers, so they had been declared the winners of the treasure hunt. Their prize was to decide what the next adventure would be.

"Let's play a game," said Arthur, who was wearing his crown. "How about hide-and-seek?"

"Ooh yes, and then let's build forts in the dungeons!" Victoria added.

Kirsty smiled at Rachel as they put on their crowns.

"Now that Elisa has her tiara, everyone has their sense of adventure back," she said with a laugh. "And adventures definitely make life more fun! I wonder what *our* next one will be?"

Rachel and Kirsty have helped Hope,
Cassidy, Anya, and Elisa find their tiaras.
Now it's time for them to help

Lizzie
the Sweet Treats Fairy!

Join their next adventure
in this special sneak peek. . . .

Royal Tea Party

"Having a tea party here in the Orangery is going to be really fun!" Rachel exclaimed to her best friend, Kirsty. "I bet that's just what the *real* princes and princesses who once lived in the Golden Palace used to do."

"I wonder if we're going to have a royal tea with cucumber sandwiches and cupcakes," Kirsty said with a smile.

"The Orangery is the perfect place for a special party!"

The Orangery was a lovely white greenhouse with huge arched windows. It stood in the grounds of the Golden Palace. Terra-cotta pots of orange, lemon, and lime trees lined the walls of the Orangery, and the air was warm and smelled like citrus. A spiral staircase in the middle of the building swept up to a wrought-iron balcony, which had spectacular views of the Golden Palace and its enormous grounds. From the balcony, Rachel and Kirsty could see the drawbridge and moat, the lake and gardens, the maze, the petting zoo, and the croquet field.

"The Golden Palace looks beautiful in the sunshine," Kirsty remarked. The palace had four high towers, one at each corner of the building, and a fifth tower, the highest one, right in the center. Flags flew on top of all five towers and their golden turrets glittered in the spring sun.

"Aren't we lucky to be here for the Royal Sleepover Camp?" Rachel smiled at Kirsty as they made their way back down the spiral staircase. "Thank you *so* much for inviting me to come."

The Golden Palace was located in the countryside near Kirsty's hometown of Wetherbury, and the girls were spending spring vacation there with a group of other kids, doing all kinds of fun and interesting activities. . . .

RAINBOW magic™

There's Magic in Every Series!

The Rainbow Fairies
The Weather Fairies
The Jewel Fairies
The Pet Fairies
The Fun Day Fairies
The Petal Fairies
The Dance Fairies
The Music Fairies
The Sports Fairies
The Party Fairies
The Ocean Fairies
The Night Fairies
The Magical Animal Fairies
The Princess Fairies

Read them all!

■ SCHOLASTIC

www.scholastic.com
www.rainbowmagiconline.com

HIT entertainment

RMFAIR

RAINBOW magic™

SPECIAL EDITION

Three Books in Each One—More Rainbow Magic Fun!

Joy the Summer Vacation Fairy

Holly the Christmas Fairy

Kylie the Carnival Fairy

Stella the Star Fairy

Shannon the Ocean Fairy

Trixie the Halloween Fairy

Gabriella the Snow Kingdom Fairy

Juliet the Valentine Fairy

Mia the Bridesmaid Fairy

Flora the Dress-Up Fairy

Paige the Christmas Play Fairy

Emma the Easter Fairy

Cara the Camp Fairy

Destiny the Rock Star Fairy

Belle the Birthday Fairy

Olympia the Games Fairy

Selena the Sleepover Fairy

Cheryl the Christmas Tree Fairy